First Experiences

Sam Starts School

Written by **Barbara Taylor Cork**

Illustrated by **Nicola Smee**

B R I M A X

This is Sam. Tomorrow is his first day at school. Mother has put out his new clothes ready for the morning.

Sam wakes up very early. He feels excited, but a little scared, too. "Why don't you take Panda with you?" says Mother. Sam thinks this is a good idea.

"Have a good day," says Father, as Sam and Mother set off for school. It's not far and Sam knows the way.

There are lots of children at school already. Sam's friend, Jonathan, waves to him. Sam is pleased to see him and waves back.

Miss Hunter, the teacher, comes to meet Sam.
She shows him where to hang his coat. There is
a different picture above each peg. Sam's peg has
a picture of a red balloon.

"Come and see what we've got in the classroom," says Miss Hunter, leading the way. Sam and his Mother follow Miss Hunter into the classroom.

"Look," says Miss Hunter, "this is your drawer. You could put Panda in here to keep him safe." Sam is very pleased. The drawer also has his name on it.

Jonathan is playing in the water trough. Sam wants to play with the water as well.
"Let's put on this apron," suggests Miss Hunter, "then you won't get your clothes wet."

"Goodbye Sam," says Mother, "I'll come and collect you at the end of school. I'll wait by the door." Sam gives Mother a big hug and waves goodbye.

After a little while, Miss Hunter calls the children. They sit on a mat and sing a song. Sam knows all the words and he sings quite loudly.

"Now it's playtime," says Miss Hunter. "Let's line up in pairs by the door. Then you can get your coats and go outside." Sam lines up with his new friend, Poppy.

Anna and Jonathan hold Miss Hunter's hands for a little while. Sam and Poppy play monsters.

The playground is very busy. There are lots of children running around and playing games.

After playtime, the children go back to their classroom. "Would you like to do some painting?" Miss Hunter asks Sam and Jonathan.
"I'm going to paint a robot," says Sam.
"I think I'll paint a dragon," says Jonathan.

Soon it's time for lunch. "Let's go and wash our hands before we eat," says Miss Hunter. "Does anyone need to go to the toilet?" she asks. "Don't forget to wash your hands afterwards," Miss Hunter reminds them.

They eat lunch in the hall. Some children have
school meals. Some children have brought
packed lunches.

Sam sits next to Poppy. He eats everything on his plate, but Poppy eats only the pasta. There's a jug of water so the children can have a drink.

After lunch, the children go out to the playground together. Sam and his new friends play tag.

Sam feels a little tired at the end of lunchtime. "Why don't you choose a book to look at?" says Miss Hunter. Sam sits on a big, soft cushion and shows Panda the pictures in his storybook.

Jonathan is playing with the bricks. "Come and see my tower," he says. Sam helps him make the tower even taller.

It will be time to go home soon. Miss Hunter asks everyone to tidy up. When everything is put away, the children sit on the mat and Miss Hunter reads them a story.

Mother is waiting by the classroom door to take Sam home. "How was your day?" she asks him. "I did a painting," he says. "Look."

Sam waves goodbye to Poppy. "That's my new friend," he says proudly. "I wonder what we'll do at school tomorrow?"